The Tyrannosaurus thought,
*In this world, strength means
everything. The strongest wins.
The strongest rules.
And I am the strongest!*

Sometimes he was violent
and mean.

"Stop, please!"
"Help!"

The Tyrannosaurus laughed.
"You are weaklings!
Weaklings are worthless.
The strongest rules,
and I am the strongest,
ha, ha, ha. . . ."

When the Tyrannosaurus was violent,
no one did anything!
When they heard his voice,
everyone trembled and hid.

"The Ty . . . Tyrannosaurus is here."
"He will hurt you if he finds you."
"Shh! Quiet. . . ."
"I'm scared. . . ."

Before they realized it, they also started thinking
that the Tyrannosaurus could do anything
he wanted to because he was the strongest.
Time passed . . .

ROARRR

The Tyrannosaurus grew old.
One day he was shuffling along on his tired old legs
when a Masiakasaurus mocked him.
"Hey, slowpoke, can you shuffle over here?
Ha, ha, ha . . . "

"Shut your mouth or I will eat you!"
the Tyrannosaurus answered,
but he couldn't catch the Masiakasaurus.

Another Masiakasaurus bit the
Tyrannosaurus's tail.

CHOMP!

"Ouch. . . stop," the Tyrannosaurus cried.
But he was old and had no strength left.
No one was scared of him anymore.

The Tyrannosaurus set off on a journey.
He wanted to go where he could be alone.
He felt a throbbing pain in his tail where the
Masiakasaurus had bitten him.

He walked for days until finally he got
tired and lay down.
Strength is what rules the world. . . .
I'm not strong anymore. . . .
I am worthless. . . .
How am I going to live from now on?
he wondered as he fell into a deep sleep.

In the morning, a voice woke him.
"Mister! Mister!"

He opened his eyes and saw a
yummy-looking baby Triceratops
right in front of him.
The Tyrannosaurus opened his mouth
and was about to gobble
the baby Triceratops,
but his tail hurt so badly
he couldn't get up.

"Mister, your tail is red and swollen.
Are you all right?"
asked the baby Triceratops.

The Triceratops stroked the
Tyrannosaurus's tail.
"You shouldn't be sleeping like this.
The strong, scary Tarbosaurus
will eat you up."
"Eat me up? ME?"

"Yup. He gave you this wound, right?
He almost ate you, didn't he?"

"No, he didn't. The Tarbosaurus
is not that strong.
There's someone stronger than him."

"Oh! Are you thinking of the Gorgosaurus?"
the Triceratops asked.

The Tyrannosaurus was dismayed.
"I'm thinking of someone who is much,
much stronger," he said.
"Someone who has jagged teeth and glaring eyes."
The Tyrannosaurus bared his teeth and
opened his eyes wide.

The baby Triceratops looked at him and said,
"Of course! I've forgotten the scariest
and strongest of all . . .

"The Tyrannosaurus!"

The Tyrannosaurus was
so happy to hear that,
he picked up the baby
Triceratops and hugged
him!

"So, the Tyrannosaurus
is the strongest
guy around?"

"Yes, he's the strongest. You look strong, mister.
But when you see the Tyrannosaurus,
you'd better run or he'll eat you up in an instant."

The Tyrannosaurus looked at the baby Triceratops.
"Have you ever seen a Tyrannosaurus?" he asked.

"Oh no! The Tyrannosaurus is very violent.
If I'd seen him he would have eaten me up!"
The baby Triceratops giggled nervously.

"That's true," the Tyrannosaurus said.

The Tyrannosaurus was about to gobble him up
when the baby Triceratops asked,
"Mister, will you meet my friends?
They'll all be so happy if you hold
them like this too."

I'm going to have a Triceratops feast today,
the Tyrannosaurus thought.

Slowly the Tyrannosaurus followed
the baby Triceratops on his old legs.

"My friends are in the woods," the baby
Triceratops said, and shouted,
"Hey! Everyone come meet my friend!"

"Wow. You look so big and strong,"
said all the little Triceratops. They'd never seen a
Tyrannosaurus before.

"Isn't he great? He just picked me up and
held me," the baby Triceratops said.

"*I* want to be held too."
All the little Triceratops hugged the Tyrannosaurus
and begged to be picked up.
The Tyrannosaurus was surprised because nothing
like this had ever happened to him before.

"No, no, guys!" said one little Triceratops."
"Even a mighty man like Mr. Rhabdodon
can get tired."
"Huh? Rhabdodon?" muttered the
Tyrannosaurus. "Rhabdodon is a stupid
weakling and only eats grass. . . . Don't these
kids know anything?"
"Besides, his tail was bitten and
he's wounded," the baby Triceratops said.

"Oh, it's true. His tail is
so swollen. . . ."
"Are you all right,
Mr. Rhabdodon?"
"We are so sorry. We didn't
know about your wound."

The little Triceratops patted the Tyrannosaurus's tail very gently. They also cared for his wound by licking it tenderly.

"All right! Why don't we all go get some red berries for Mr. Rhabdodon so that he can heal more quickly?" the baby Triceratops said.

The little Triceratops started ramming their horns against the red-berry tree.
BAM! BAM!
The tree didn't budge, but the little Triceratops did not stop.

They charged at the tree again and again.
Soon their horns started hurting, but they did not give up.

BAM! BAM!
The sound echoed in the quiet woods.
They're doing this for me,
the Tyrannosaurus realized.

He was so moved that
he got tears in his eyes.

"K-kids, that's enough.
I'll show you how."
CRACK! SNAP!

The red berries showered down like rain.

"Wow, that's amazing!"
"You are fantastic, Mr. Rhabdodon!"

The kindness of the little Triceratops touched the Tyrannosaurus.

"I want to be strong like you, mister!"
said one little Triceratops, and the others agreed.
"We want to be JUST LIKE YOU."
"I bet you can even beat a mean Tyrannosaurus."
"Yeah, the one who says,
'Power and strength mean everything.'"

"Strength means everything. . . . Power is . . . ,"
the Tyrannosaurus mumbled,
popping red berries into his mouth.

"Well, kids, it isn't so.
What's truly important is . . ."

The Tyrannosaurus was interrupted by a voice.

"Well, well. You've got a lot of yummy-looking
Triceratops babies with you. Why don't you give us some?"
Two Giganotosauruses were glaring
at the Tyrannosaurus with blazing eyes.
The little Triceratops trembled and clung to
the Tyrannosaurus.
"Help us, mister!" they cried.

The Tyrannosaurus stared back at the Giganotosauruses and growled.
"GRRRR!"

Then he held the little Triceratops firmly in his arms,
curled his body around them, and did not move.
"Give us those babies!"
The Giganotosauruses bit the Tyrannosaurus's tail,
which was already swollen and red.
CHOMP! They bit his back. **CHOMP!**
And they used their claws to tear into the Tyrannosaurus's body.

"I'll protect you. . . .
I'll protect you all . . . ," the Tyrannosaurus said.
He held the little Triceratops and kept them safe.

And as he endured the violence, he murmured,
"I finally understand. . . . Remember this, kids.
It's not being strong that is important.
What's most important is . . ."

The Tyrannosaurus held the little Triceratops in his arms and did not move. After a long time the Giganotosauruses went away, and the Tyrannosaurus fell over. Carefully the Triceratops crawled out from under him.

"Mister? Mister?"

"Are you all right?"

"Umm . . . I'm a little tired so I'm going to sleep here . . . You have to go home," the Tyrannosaurus said softly, and he closed his eyes.

"Okay. Good night," said the little Triceratops, and they headed home.

All except the baby Triceratops who was the first to meet the Tyrannosaurus. "But, the most important thing? What were you going to say after that?" he asked. The Tyrannosaurus did not reply.

A large shooting star blazed across the sky.

Many, many years went by.
A father Triceratops and his babies were eating
red berries in the woods.
Two Giganotosauruses suddenly approached,
drool dripping from their mouths.

"Arghhh!"
The father Triceratops curled his body around
his babies and did not move at all, no matter
how violent the Giganotosauruses became.
He remembered how the Tyrannosaurus had
protected him and his friends.

Night fell.
The Giganotosauruses gave up and went
away because the Triceratops father was
as hard as a rock and never moved.
"Are you all right, Dad?"
"The Giganotosauruses ran away from us,
didn't they? You were great!"
"Dad, you are a strong guy.
Why didn't you beat them up?"

"Listen, kids. Violence isn't the answer.
There is something more powerful than strength,
and more precious too. That is love. Love is stronger than
violence. A truly strong guy who broke this tree once gave
me that love . . . ," the father Triceratops said.
One of his babies stared at the tree then looked at
his father and said,
"Will you give me that love? I want that love."

I WANT THAT LOVE

Bokunimo sono ai wo kudasai © 2006 Tatsuya Miyanishi
All rights reserved.

Translation by Mariko Shii Gharbi
English editing by Simone Kaplan

Library of Congress Cataloging-in-Publication Data

Names: Miyanishi, Tatsuya, 1956- author, illustrator. | Gharbi, Marido Shii, translator. | Kaplan,
    Simone, editor.
Title: I want that love / Tatsuya Miyanishi ; translation by Mariko Shii Gharbi ; English editing by
    Simone Kaplan.
Other titles: Bokunimo sono ai wo kudasai. English
Description: New York : Museyon, [2016] | Series: Tyrannosaurus series ; book 3 | "Originally
    published in Japan in 2006 by POPLAR Publishing Co., Ltd."--Title page verso. |
    Summary: "I Want that Love" tells the story of how a violent strong guy comes to realize
    the power of love. It is the thrid book in Tatsuya Miyanishi's Tyrannosaurus series,
    which explores friendship and love, caring and connection, and delivers lots of surprises
    in a bold, brightly depicted world of dinosaurs.--Publisher.
Identifiers: ISBN: 978-1-940842-14-1 | LCCN: 2016913182
Subjects: LCSH: Tyrannosaurus rex--Juvenile fiction. | Triceratops--Juvenile fiction. |
    Dinosaurs--Juvenile fiction. | Love--Juvenile fiction. | Friendship--Juvenile fiction. |
    Bullies--Juvenile fiction. | CYAC: Tyrannosaurus rex--Fiction. | Triceratops--Fiction. |
    Disosaurs--Fiction. | Love--Fiction. | Friendship--Fiction. | Bullies--Fiction. | BISAC:
    JUVENILE FICTION / Animals / Dinosaurs & Prehistoric Creatures.
Classification: LCC: PZ7.M699575 I183 2016 | DDC: [E]--dc23

Published in the United States and Canada by:
Museyon Inc.
1177 Avenue of the Americas, 5th Floor
New York, NY 10036

Museyon is a registered trademark.
Visit us online at www.museyon.com

Originally published in Japan in 2006 by POPLAR Publishing Co., Ltd.
English translation rights arranged with POPLAR Publishing Co., Ltd.

Printed in China

ISBN 9781940842141